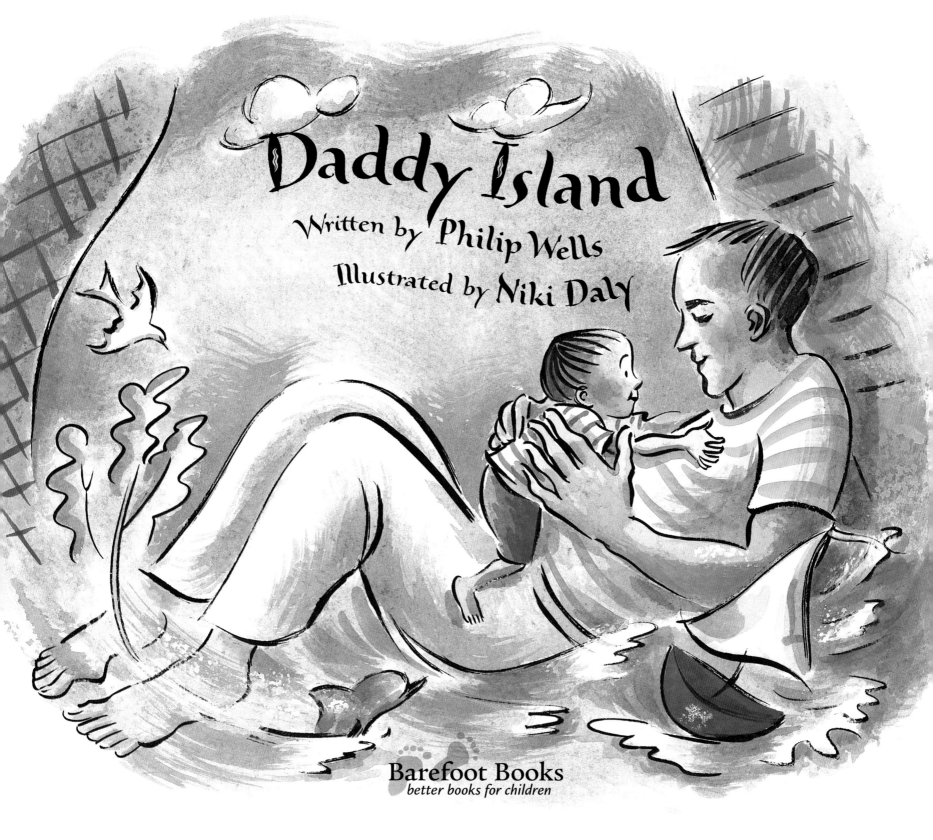

Daddy Island

Written by Philip Wells

Illustrated by Niki Daly

Barefoot Books
better books for children

I am a tree on Daddy Island

I can stretch till I'm very very tall.

I'm amazingly high — I'd better not fall.

Across the forest I send my call,

I am a tree and I'm taller than tall.

I am a storm on Daddy Island

I can shout very very loud.

Louder than the rackle of a thundercloud!

I am very angry and wild and proud.

I am a storm and I'm louder than loud!

I am a bird on Daddy Island

I can soar very very high.

Under my wings the world glides by.

I am a king in the kingdom of the sky.

I am a bird and I'm higher than high.

I am a crab on Daddy Island

I can move very very fast

Quick as a zing or a fizz or a blast!

One little blink and I've whizzed right past.

I am a crab and I'm faster than fast.

I am a rock on Daddy Island

I can stay very very still.

Still as a mountain, still as a hill.

Strong and steady, steady and still.

I am a rock and I'm stiller than still.

I can shrink till I'm very very small.

I can curl up in a tiny little ball.

And I can creep and I can crawl.

I am an ant and I'm smaller than small.

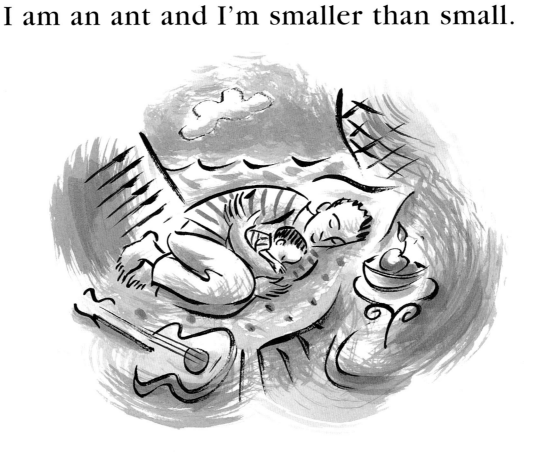

I am a star on Daddy Island

I can shine very very bright.

I am a sun burning in the night.

Watch me flicker like candlelight.

I am a star and I'm brighter than bright.

I am a snail on Daddy Island

I can move, but I'm very very slow.

I am so relaxed wherever I go.

I'm not in any hurry, you know.

I am a snail and I'm slower than slow.

I am a bear on Daddy Island

I am fierce but I'm very very loving.

I soon get tired of pushing and shoving.

I can feel it when your heart is moving.

I am a bear and I'm very very loving.

I am the sand on Daddy Island

I can whisper very very quietly.

I listen to the waves and the wind in the tree.

I am very very soft and I lie so quietly.

I am the sand in the starlight by the sea.

I am a dream on Daddy Island

Barefoot Books
better books for children

At Barefoot Books, we celebrate art and story with books that open the hearts and minds of children from all walks of life, inspiring them to read deeper, search further, and explore their own creative gifts. Taking our inspiration from many different cultures, we focus on themes that encourage independence of spirit, enthusiasm for learning, and acceptance of other traditions. Thoughtfully prepared by writers, artists, and storytellers from all over the world, our products combine the best of the present with the best of the past to educate our children as the caretakers of tomorrow.

www.barefootbooks.com

Barefoot Books
37 West 17th Street
4th Floor East
New York, NY 10011

First published in the United States of America in 2001
by Barefoot Books, Inc.

This book has been printed on 100% acid-free paper
The illustrations were prepared in brush, ink and watercolor

Design by Jennie Hoare, England
Calligraphy by Andrew van der Merwe, South Africa
Typeset in 22pt Garamond Book
Color separation by Bright Arts, Singapore
Printed and bound in Hong Kong / China by
South China Printing Co. (1988) Ltd

1 3 5 7 9 8 6 4 2

Library of Congress Cataloging-in-Publication Data

Wells, Philip.
  Daddy Island / written by Philip Wells ; illustrated by Niki Daly.
    p. cm.
  Summary: Daddy's body makes a wonderful play island for a young boy.
  ISBN 1-84148-197-1
  [1. Fathers and sons–Fiction. 2. Play–Fiction. 3. Stories in rhyme.]
  I. Daly, Niki, ill. II. Title.
  PZ8.3.W4647 Dad 2001
  [E]–dc21

00-010727

For Laurence and Daddy, with love — P. V. W.
For my son Leo, from Niki with love — N. D.